Iggy The Introvert

By:

D.A. Armstrong

D.Arrot

Illustrations By:

S.P. Armstrong

S. Armstrong

See how many flies you can count in the pictures.
Answer at the end of the book.

It was a hot day in May.
The students couldn't wait to play.

Another hour had to pass
before they could leave class.

"Quiet please. Settle down",
said Mr. Green, holding a crown.

"It's time for the poem contest,
and whoever is the best,
will win a treat.
Something sweet to beat the heat!"

"Now who wants to start?"
"I do", said Lily. "I have a poem from the heart"

"Okay begin,"
said Mr. Green with a grin.

"This is about my really good friend,
who I hope you will better understand by
my poems end."

"There once was a frog named Iggy,
That everyone thought was a little wiggy.
He was quiet as a mouse,
And rarely left his house
But to him it was no biggie."

"His Mom says he's an introvert.
I asked him if it hurt.
He said, 'No in reality,
It's just my personality.'
Then we shared some frozen fly yogurt."

"Some think that he is being rude,
And has a bad attitude.
Though his eyes maybe glistening
He is always listening.
Iggy really is a cool dude!"

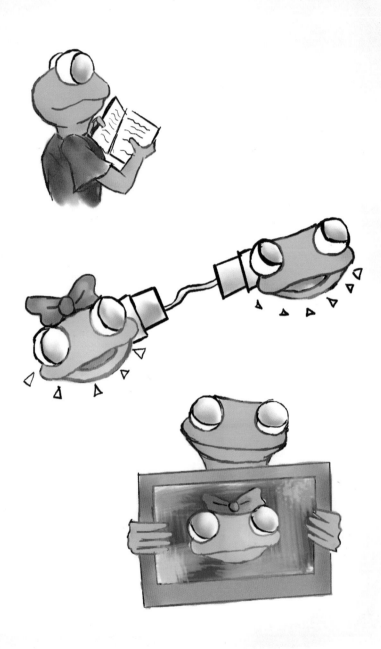

"Sometimes he likes to be alone,
Or just talk on the phone.
Instead of taking part
He practices his art
A talent I wish I could own."

"Large groups make Iggy weary.
And sometimes a little teary,
But after a rest,
He's at his best.
And back to cheery, cheery!"

"So if you are patient and kind,
I know you will find,
Iggy can be a great friend,
Loyal to the end,
With the most creative mind."

Mr. Green said, "That was wonderful, really sweet.
Now please go back to your seat"

Iggy turned red,
and covered his head.

He was proud of Lily,
but felt a little silly.

"Iggy, I'm sorry if I have ever made you
feel bad", said Jim
"We are all going after class for a swim."
"Do you want to come too?
It's okay if you don't, it's up to you."

"That sounds great,
But I cannot stay very late"

They all had a lot of fun.
Many new friendships had just begun.

The next day Lily hopped with pride up to her friend Iggy who was reading outside.

"Do you want to hear something neat? My poem won! Would you like some of my treat?"

With a smile and a look,
Iggy went back to reading his book.

Number of flies:

50

Denise A. Armstrong

As a little girl Denise loved to listen to and read Dr. Seuss books. The rhythm of the rhymes made reading fun. She chose to use rhyming in her first book *Iggy the Introvert* (available on Amazon) in the hopes that others would enjoy it too. She was thrilled when her daughter Shaelyn agreed to do the illustrations.

Like many introverts Denise enjoys reading, listening to music, watching movies and painting. She was born and continues to live in Newmarket, ON with her daughter. You can follow Denise on the following social media accounts.

 @nmktdenart facebook.com/DArtpaintings

Shaelyn P. Armstrong

Shaelyn, an aspiring artist, was thrilled when her mother presented the idea of a children's book to her as a summer project. The experimentation with the art as well as the collaboration with her mother was a unique experience she'll never forget.

As someone who has experienced first hand how ignorance about introverted people can affect one's life Shaelyn was more than happy to help out.

Shaelyn enjoys reading and drawing in her free time and loves living in Newmarket with her family and friends.

 @artisbellator